AMIRA'S
SUITCASE

*To all the children—all over the world—who have
ever shared their story with me. ~ V C*

*For Coral, my dear friend who always
fills my world with sunshine. ~ N J*

American edition published in 2022
by New Frontier Publishing Europe Ltd
www.newfrontierpublishing.us

First published in Great Britain in 2021
by New Frontier Publishing Europe Ltd,
Uncommon, 126 New King's Rd, London SW6 4LZ
www.newfrontierpublishing.co.uk

Distributed in the United States and Canada by Lerner Publishing Group Inc.
241 First Avenue North, Minneapolis, MN 55401 USA
www.lernerbooks.com

Library of Congress Cataloging-in-Publication data is available.

ISBN: 978-1-913639-77-8

Designed by Verity Clark

Printed in China

10 9 8 7 6 5 4 3 2 1

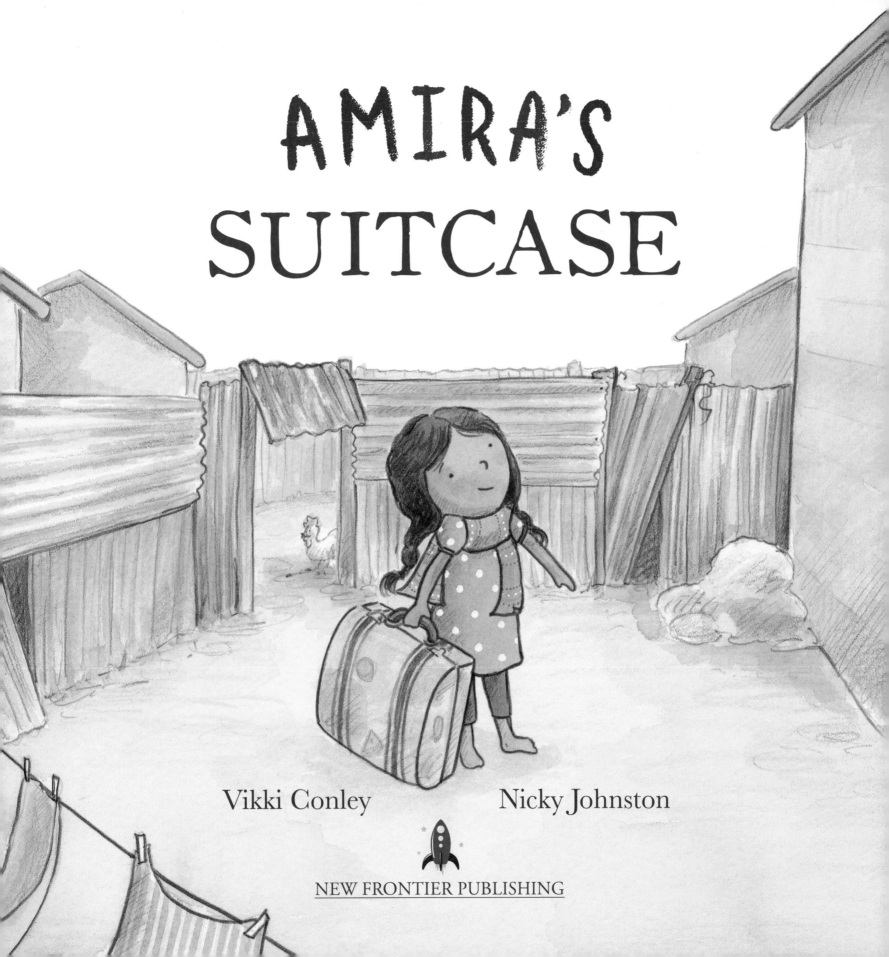

AMIRA'S SUITCASE

Vikki Conley   Nicky Johnston

NEW FRONTIER PUBLISHING

It was growing in the corner of a
suitcase when Amira first saw it.

Amira had been looking
for a place to hide.

"I won't hurt you," she said.

Later that day, Amira visited her new friend.
"Perhaps I'll leave the lid open for you," she said.
"Momma says fresh air will help you grow."

Amira smiled at the sprout.
She felt something blossom
deep inside her.

The next day, Amira hid
behind the suitcase.

She saw a finger of sunlight
reaching for the small pile of dirt.

"Here, I'll help you,"
said Amira.

"And tomorrow I'll
bring you something."

Amira returned with a broken coconut shell.

"You look thirsty. I get thirsty too. Let's share."

Water trickled down
Amira's hand.

She felt a bud of warmth
flicker in her belly.

Amira smiled as the sprout glowed in the sun.
"You remind me of green pears.
Will you be a pear tree? I miss our pear tree."

That night, Amira climbed through green leaves. She reached for a ripe pear.

The next day, Amira met Nala. "Come meet my friend," said Amira, pointing to the sprout.

"I used to have a friend like
that," said Nala.
"Me too," said Amira.

The memory made her feel cozy inside.

When Nala came again, she uncurled Amira's fingers. Amira's hand quivered and tingled.

"This could be a friend, for your
new friend," said Nala.
"Don't let it blow away."

"Grow up, up, up to the sky."
Amira filled her lungs and sang.

"I don't think you're a pear tree, because
you don't smell like a pear. You remind me
of something else."

That night, Amira dreamed of a sparkling pool.
It smelled fresh and sweet, like her momma's mint tea.

At breakfast time, Tien cupped his hand
to Amira's ear.

"I hear you're keeping some treasures safe," he said. "Here, take this."

Amira felt the warmth of the seed travel all the way to her toes.

"This can be your corner," said
Amira to the seed.

"You can be the little brother."

"We'll look after you,"
said Amira.

Amira stood up.

She felt **taller**.

In fact, Amira felt like she could
almost touch the sky.

Together, they dug a new home for the plants.

Together, they smiled at the flourishing leaves.

And together they climbed
up, up, up . . .

. . . toward the sun.